HERE COMES THE CAT! / СЮДА ИДЕТ КОТ!

FRANK ASCH / VLADIMIR VAGIN

McSWEENEY'S McMULLENS

www.mcsweeneys.net

In Russian,

СЮДА ИДЕТ КОТ!

means *Here Comes the Cat!*
and is pronounced
syu-DAH ee-DYOT KOT!

To my son,
DEVIN

FRANK ASCH

To my daughter,
ANASTASIA

—VLADIMIR VAGIN

I LIVE FAR away from America, on the other part of the globe in Moscow. But Frank Asch and I made this book together, as if we lived on the same street, just across the fence. It is the first book in the world designed by an American and painted by a Russian.

There is an old Russian proverb: "One wise head is good; two are better." As you can see, a Russian and an American can both be good friends and do one job. Turn the pages of our book and read about the big cat that came to a mouse settlement, and how it turned out that there was absolutely nothing to be frightened about.

—Vladimir Vagin, 1989

WORKING WITH VLADIMIR across the great distance that separates our two countries has been an exciting and gratifying experience. It began in 1986 when we both attended a Soviet/American children's book symposium. A few nights after the symposium I woke with a dream that was the basic idea for *Here Comes the Cat!*

Vladimir speaks very little English, and I speak no Russian at all; but as we worked together, translator/couriers flying our sketches and notes back and forth, we got to know one another, not just as artists, but as fellow human beings and friends.

—Frank Asch, 1989

IN THE YEARS since *Here Comes the Cat!* was first published, I've permanently moved to the United States and illustrated fourteen more children's books. My wife and I live in Burlington, Vermont. I am currently painting large-scale watercolors inspired by the landscape surrounding Lake Champlain.

—Vladimir Vagin, 2011

IT'S BEEN OVER twenty years since Vladimir and I created *Here Comes The Cat!* The world may not have changed very much during that time, but we have become the best of friends. That for me is the huge piece of cheese at the end of the story.

—Frank Asch, 2011